THE CASE OF CURSED GOLD COIN

BY

Ankur Baranwal

Table of Contents

CHAPTER 1 — ARRIVAL OF THE UNEXPECTED

Out of many cases of Mr. Marple, the case of the lost gold coin is one peculiar one.

It all started one day, Mr. Marple and I were having tea in the morning, all of a sudden, a man entered our house. He was sweating and was scared.

“Mr. Marple where are you?” asked the stranger.

“I am right here Mr.….”

“I am Mr. Harrington from 434 Avenue Street, California.”

“Well, I assume that you have a case for me and that to an important one.”

“How were you able to predict that?”

“Well, it’s quite simple, it’s 7 in the morning people usually sleep during winters at this time.”

“Oh, I see.”

“Now leave all this talk and tell me about your case, Mr. Harrington.”

“It all began when three days ago when the heritage of our family went missing,

The only leftover thing of my great grandfather, GOLD COIN OF QUEENS.”

“So didn’t you report this to the police?”

“The police said that it might have been misplaced by us but it is nowhere to be found.”

“So, except for being the emotional value does that thing have any other value, like commercial value?”

“Yes, Mr. Marple it is worth 9 million dollars”

“Well now that interesting, can you tell me when was it the last time you saw?”

“It was three days ago just before the reunion had just begun.”

“What kind of reunion?”

“It was the reunion of our family.”

“Was every present there?”

“Yes, except one the only child of my older brother.”

“Well now that’s it, I will myself come to your house to investigate till that time tell everyone to not leave the city without any information and telling me.

CHAPTER 2 — INVESTIGATION AT QUEENS MANSION

The next day I and Mr. Marple went to the Queens Mansion.

There we met an old man.

"Who might you be?" asked the old man.

"I am Mr. Marple and this is my assistant, Hazelton"

"Oh, I see you must be the detective that Harrington must have called."

"Yes…"

"Please follow me."

We went inside the mansion. The mansion was built in the classic style but lacked much maintenance.

"Please wait here I will go and tell Master Harrington."

The old man went inside a room and suddenly a crash sound came from upstairs. We went up. A mirror was broken, and a terrified woman sat on the bed looking at the broken mirror.

"Are you alright Miss?" asked Marple.

"S…s…somebody threw a stone from the outside," said the woman stammering in fear.

We went near the window and found a paper near it.

"Something's written on it, I will read:

This is the first attack, but more will follow dangerously"

"What…?"

"Ah, Mr. Harrington don't worry the culprit will be caught soon"

"The fear is not because of this but about the prophecy…"

"Harrington, what is this prophecy you speak of? Tell us more, please."

"The prophecy or I should say a curse…"

CHAPTER 3— PROPHECY OR CURSE

"It's more like a curse than a prophecy…" said Mr. Harrington stammering.

"More like a curse, how?"

"The story all began during the time of my grandfather's father. He was in a jungle when he learned of a new relic, a coin that can bring good fortune to anyone who has it. As he searched for it, he found that it was protected by an ancient clan, so he killed all of them and returned with the coin. However, it is said that he also had a curse on him, that anyone who touches it or goes near it will die."

"Is it the same coin that has been stolen?"

"No, that coin had been hidden in this mansion for longer than I remember but many tries had been made to steal it."

"So, it explains the stone attack and the warning but it doesn't explain how is it related to the coin that was stolen?"

"The coin that was stolen was made from the treasure that was brought with the cursed gold coin."

"Ok… now tell me about the night when the coin was stolen."

"That night we were having a reunion and all people were present there except one, the son of my elder brother Andrew. He is the one who has not contacted any member of our family for years."

"Was there any special reason for the reunion?"

"Yes, it was to announce the start of my new company."

"Was anyone else present there other than your family mem…"

"Master Harrington master Harrington," shouted a servant.

"What is it?"

"It's very bad sir."

"Why, what happened?"

“A man came to me and told me to tell you that if Mr. Marple pursues this further, the Queen family will end."

“Well, this makes things interesting” exclaimed Marple.

“What should we do, Mr. Marple?” Harrington screamed in fear.

“It looks like that the culprit is a sharp one…, I think that if I stay here for a while, it might prove dangerous but don’t you fear Hazelton will stay with you. Hazelton will you please come with me for a moment."

I and Marple move out of the mansion, where he tells me to be cautioned at all times and to write him a letter of his investigations as soon as possible.

CHAPTER 4— HAZELTON'S INVESTIGATION

Marple left the same day and I started my investigations the next day. I found all about the Andrew boy and was shocked to hear that after the death of his father he disappeared and the address he gave is in India.

"So, you are saying that Andrew's mother died after one year of his birth."

"Yes, Mr. Hazelton."

"Oh, please call me Hazelton."

"Breakfast is ready masters."

We went to the dining hall where I met the rest of the family.

There was Mr. Oliver, an architect working in England, followed by Mrs. Filch and her son Shino, and the rest of the family was out enjoying their visit to California.

"Mr. Harrington would give me a tour of this mansion after breakfast?"

"Yes, sure."

After having breakfast, Mr. Harrington and I went to take a tour of the mansion, and Mrs. Filch and her son went to meet the rest of the family.

There were several rooms in the mansion but the room where the coin was kept was secured.

There were several guards present there and the room was locked with four locks and the keys were present with Mr. Harrington. Around four to five guards were present inside the room and the coin case was kept in an unbreakable glass.

“There’s no way some would have gone through such tight security and have stolen the coin.”

“That’s the reason why I contacted Mr. Marple.”

“You did the right thing, Mr. Harrington this case is much more mysterious than expected.”

After looking around the mansion we went into the picture room where Mr. Harrington told me about his ancestors and the leftover members of the family.

“Leftover members?” I asked.

“Yes, Mr. Hazelton most of the members of the family have died but the reason for their death is very odd.”

“What do you mean by ‘odd’?”

“See, my father Harrington the Third was killed in a car wreck in a forest, my uncle Frizz was bitten by a snake, and my other uncle Mathew drowned while swimming. Uncle Frizz was the father of Andrew.”

“Well, that’s very odd.”

After talking for a while, we went to eat dinner. The whole family was present there.

During the night I heard someone talking outside my window.

CHAPTER 5— HAZELTON'S INVESTIGATION-II

It had been a few days since I arrived at the Queens' Mansion, I found a lot about the family members but I was unable to find out how did the thief enter the coin room.

I wrote many letters to Marple telling him about the things that happened and he told me to keep a close eye on all the members especially Mr. Harrington.

“Breakfast is ready Mr. Hazelton”

“Are you the only butler that the whole mansion has?”

“Apparently, yes.”

It was no use, keeping an eye on Mr. Harrington he was always in his room sleeping most of the time and made his appearance very rarely. We went to the dining hall it was to my surprise that all members of the family were present there. One of them asked about Mr. Marple and I answered that he was busy in some other case, after hearing this Mr. Harrington became tense.

"Please don't be tensed, Mr. Harrington," said Marple.

"Mr. Marple, is that you?"

"Yes, my dear Hazelton."

Everyone sitting over there was surprised.

After having breakfast, I and Marple went into my room.

"So have you found about the person who was talking outside your window?"

"No, but I think I wrote what I have heard in one of my letters."

"Yes, it's right."

"Marple, I heard regular sounds coming from the outside, but when I went outside to investigate, I couldn't figure out what was happening."

"No worries, Hazelton now I am here we will see today what is happening over here."

Chapter 6— Voices Outside

Marple and I woke that night till mid but we heard no sounds. Many days passed but no sounds came it looked like the person making sounds must have become cautious. Our prime suspect Harrington didn't do anything suspicious at all, so we decided to get some look around.

We met the neighbours. We got to know that Mr. Harrington didn't live here but came here just a few months before the reunion and he started some renovations in the mansion. We interrogated Mr. Harrington but nothing came good out of it.

That night around eleven a creaking sound came from the living room.

I and Marple went into the living room to see what was happening, we found a window opened.

“It must be the wind.”

“No, Hazelton the wind is not that strong that it will open the window.”

“Let’s go and see Marple.”

We went out but it was so dark that we were unable to see anything so we both went inside the house.

The next we told Mr. Harrington about it.

"Has anything like this happened before?" asked Marple.

"No, nothing like this has ever happened before."

"We must inform the police about all this."

"Yes, you are right Mr. Marple"

"Hazelton, go and inform the police about all this."

It took me hours to do what Marple had ordered me but when I came back the whole family was looking tense even Marple was tense.

CHAPTER 7— THE UNEXPECTED INCIDENT

"What's the matter Marple, why is everyone so tense?" I asked.

Marple and others went aside and there lay a dead body.

"What is all this?"

"It's the body of a maid."

"There's also this note that was founded near the dead body Hazelton, I fear that if this case is not finished soon there will be more incidents happening like this."

"So, what should we do now Marple?"

"For now, we should take a leave from this mansion, let's go Hazelton."

I and Marple went to the nearest hotel and there I asked him whether he knew this was going to happen or who the culprit is.

"It's not that simple Hazelton, we don't have enough proof about anyone to prove them guilty and as far the murder is concerned it is the work of the person who threw the stone that day."

"So, we don't have any clues yet."

Knock… Knock…

"Who's there?"

"Room service, I have a letter for… Mr. Marple."

We took the letter and Marple read it.

It looked:

Mr. Marple, I know that many incidents have happened since the time you took this case. I am your and Queens family well-wisher so I am requesting you to leave this case and return to your home else no one knows what might happen to all.

“It’s another threat letter.”

“No, Hazelton it’s not a threat letter it looks that its writer was scared and wrote it in a hurry just look how it looks.”

I took a look at it and found that Marple was right.

"It also gives a clue of the culprit Hazelton."

"Really?"

"Yes, only the Queens family knows that we are in this hotel and the person writing this must know something about the culprit and is a user of strong perfume."

I found Marple's observation quite right. We decided to leave the hotel and end this case once and for all

tomorrow in our investigations.

CHAPTER 8— THE FINAL INVESTIGATION

The next day we went to Queens mansion and started interrogating all people, out of all of them only three became suspects.

"So, Mrs. Harrison from when have you known about the value of the gold coin?"

"Are you suspecting me Mr. Marple…(sob) I thought that you are a gentleman…(sob) blaming a lady like me for stealing…(sob).”

“Don’t try to act innocent in front of me Mrs. Harrison.”

Mrs. Harrison was shocked after hearing such hard words from Marple.

“Well, I thought that you would be flattered by that sobbing but you… leave it, I am not the culprit that’s for sure.”

“Okay, then you may take your leave now.”

Mrs. Harrison takes her to leave.

"Why did you allow her to take leave?"

"It was obvious that she was not the thief because she said confidently. So, who's next?"

"It's, Mrs. Norris."

I called Mrs. Norris and Marple was shocked.

"Were you the one who wrote the letter?"

"Which… le… le… letter… are you talking about?"

"It's simple you are wearing the same perfume that was on the letter."

"Okay, you got me."

"So, do you know who is the culprit?"

"No, I don't but I know that he is the one who talks late at night."

"Okay, then you may go now."

Mrs. Norris returned and then Marple asked me to call Mr. Smith Queens.

"Mr. Smith Queens, are you the culprit."

"What do you mean Mr. Marple? I am a well-reputed businessman."

“Yes, and your business is going into loss and you have a debt of one million, if I am correct.”

“How… how did you know this?”

“I also know that you came to California with Mr. Harrington.”

“Yes, it is true but it doesn’t prove anything.”

“Oh, I know but I believe that this is your pendant.”

“Where did you find it?”

“Near the dead body, YOU ARE THE CULPRIT SMITH QUEENS OR

SHOULD I SAY ANDREW QUEENS."

"What… oh well it looks like I am busted."

Smith took his mask off and all of us were shocked after seeing what was behind that mask… it was Andrew Queens!!

"Now will you please tell us all the story behind all this Andrew?"

"It all began when my father Frizz was thrown out of the family, I decided to take revenge on all of them. I killed many but then my company began to get into losses and my father also died but while dying he told me about this cursed gold coin and its worth. It was then when I kill Smith Queens and took his face coming here with Harrington and then I stole the coin by replacing it with a wax one. I planned to leave this country before anyone could notice but the guards were very observant."

"You didn't tell why you killed the maid?"

"Have patience Marple, I was always out because of your assistant but then too that maid heard me talking to the seller one night and saw me so I had to kill her but how did you know about me."

"It's quite simple, the night when we went out searching for you, I found this pendant and from then onwards I started my research. I found that Smith Queens had died two to three weeks before the reunion. After learning about this I started searching for you and luckily, I found your company's website which helped to get information about you. Now tell where have you hidden the coin."

"It's in my bank account but you will never be able to open it."

Andrew swallowed a poison capsule and died. I and Marple returned to our home and the Queens were happy that their heritage was safe.

9 798885 690829

Printed by Libri Plureos GmbH in Hamburg, Germany